19
J

MACHINES ★ AT WORK

CONCRETE MIXERS

BY JEAN EICK

THE CHILD'S WORLD® · MANKATO, MINNESOTA

The Child's World®

JUL 17 2007

Published in the United States of America by The Child's World®
1980 Lookout Drive • Mankato, MN 56003-1705
800-599-READ • www.childsworld.com

PHOTO CREDITS

© Chris Pancewicz/Alamy: 19
© David M. Budd Photography: 8, 11 (inset), 12, 15
© David R. Frazier Photolibrary, Inc./Alamy: 16
© iStockphoto.com/Chad Truemper: cover, 2
© iStockphoto.com/Tony Tremblay: 4, 20
© Lester Lefkowitz/Getty Images: 7
© Robert Pernell/BigStockPhoto.com: 3, 11 (main)

ACKNOWLEDGMENTS

The Child's World®: Mary Berendes, Publishing Director;
Katherine Stevenson, Editor

The Design Lab: Kathleen Petelinsek, Design and Page Production

LIBRARY OF CONGRESS CATALOGING-IN-PUBLICATION DATA

Eick, Jean, 1947–
  Concrete mixers / by Jean Eick.
    p. cm. — (Machines at work)
  Includes bibliographical references and index.
  ISBN 1-59296-829-5 (library bound : alk. paper)
  1. Concrete mixers—Juvenile literature. I. Title. II. Series.
  TA439.E33 2007
  624.1'834—dc22   2006023287

 # Contents

This concrete mixer truck is at a building site.
The workers are using concrete in the building.

What are concrete mixers?

Concrete mixer trucks stir and carry **concrete**. Concrete is almost like stone. It is used for building many things. It is used in making sidewalks, basements, walls, and roads.

5

How is concrete made?

Concrete is made by mixing water, **cement**, sand, and small stones. The wet cement acts like paste. It holds the sand and stones together. As the mixture sits, it gets hard. It also gets very strong.

concrete

This concrete mixer truck is pouring concrete. Can you see the crossed metal bars? These bars make the concrete even stronger.

cab

This concrete mixer truck has a powerful engine. The engine is in front of the cab.

What are the parts of a concrete mixer?

Some parts of concrete mixer trucks look like other trucks. The driver sits in a **cab**. The truck has an **engine**. The engine makes power that moves the truck. The driver uses the steering wheel to turn the truck.

The back looks much different from other trucks! A big **drum** holds the concrete. The drum turns around and around. As the drum turns, big **blades** inside stir the concrete.

blades

drum

Concrete mixer trucks have lots of wheels. That helps them carry heavy loads. How many wheels does this truck have?

chute

This worker is putting the truck's chute together.
Then he will point it where the concrete needs to go.

How are concrete mixers used?

A concrete mixer truck brings concrete where workers need it. The truck slowly backs up. Workers pull out the truck's **chute**. They place it where they want the concrete to go.

To mix the concrete, the drum turned one way. Now it is time to pour the concrete. The drum spins the other way. The blades push the concrete out instead of mixing it.

14

Blades push the wet concrete out of the drum. Then the concrete slides down the chute.

One worker puts the chute where the concrete needs to go. The workers must move fast. They must finish before the concrete hardens.

The concrete pours down the chute. Workers use tools to push the concrete into place. They work quickly. They must hurry before the concrete gets hard.

17

At last, all the concrete is out of the truck. The workers put the chute back into place. The concrete mixer leaves. It is ready for its next job.

18

This worker is spraying the truck with water. He is cleaning off the rest of the concrete. He does not want concrete to harden on the truck!

This truck has brought concrete to workers on a city street.

Are concrete mixers useful?

Concrete is used all over the world. It is used in all kinds of building. Concrete mixers are a big help for mixing and carrying concrete. They are very useful!

 # Glossary

blades (BLAYDZ) Blades are things that are broad, flat, and often thin.

cab (KAB) A machine's cab is the area where the driver sits.

cement (suh-MENT) Cement is a fine dust made from ground-up rocks.

chute (SHOOT) A chute is a slide.

concrete (KON-kreet) Concrete is a mixture of water, cement, sand, and small stones.

drum (DRUM) A drum is a bin for holding something.

engine (EN-jun) An engine is a machine that makes something move.

 Books

Brill, Marlene. *Concrete Mixers*. Minneapolis, MN: Lerner
Publications, 2007.

Dussling, Jennifer, and Courtney (illustrator). *Construction Trucks*.
New York: Grosset & Dunlap, 1998.

Froeb, Lori, and Tom LaPadula (illustrator). *Super Concrete Mixer*.
Pleasantville, NY: Reader's Digest Children's Books, 2005.

Web Sites

Visit our Web site for lots of links about concrete mixers:
http://www.childsworld.com/links
Note to parents, teachers, and librarians: We routinely check our Web links
to make sure they're safe, active sites—so encourage your readers to check
them out!

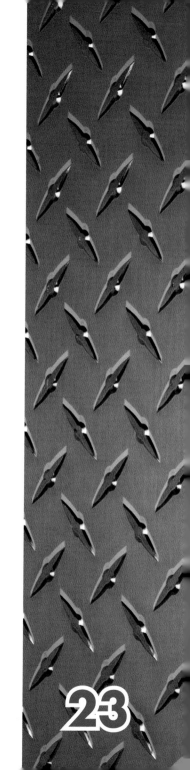

 # Index

 # About the Author

Jean Eick has written over 200 books for children over the past forty years. She has written biographies, craft books, and many titles on nature and science. Jean enjoys hiking in the mountains, reading, and doing volunteer work.

24